Dear Parents and Educators,

Welcome to Penguin Young Readers! As parents and educators, you know that each child develops at his or her own pace—in terms of speech, critical thinking, and, of course, reading. Penguin Young Readers recognizes this fact. As a result, each Penguin Young Readers book is assigned a traditional easy-to-read level (1–4) as well as a Guided Reading Level (A–P). Both of these systems will help you choose the right book for your child. Please refer to the back of each book for specific leveling information. Penguin Young Readers features esteemed authors and illustrators, stories about favorite characters, fascinating nonfiction, and more!

Max & Ruby: Max's Bug

LEVEL **2**

GUIDED
READING
LEVEL **F**

This book is perfect for a **Progressing Reader** who:
- can figure out unknown words by using picture and context clues;
- can recognize beginning, middle, and ending sounds;
- can make and confirm predictions about what will happen in the text; and
- can distinguish between fiction and nonfiction.

Here are some **activities** you can do during and after reading this book:
- Make Connections: In this story, Max takes care of his bug by feeding her and bringing her to the vet when she's sick. If you had a pet, how else would you take care of it?
- Sight Words: Sight words are frequently used words that readers must know just by looking at them. They are known instantly, on sight. Knowing these words helps children develop into efficient readers. As you read the story, have the child point out the sight words below.

any	her	his	of	put
fly	him	let	over	what

Remember, sharing the love of reading with a child is the best gift you can give!

—Sarah Fabiny, Editorial Director
  Penguin Young Readers program

*Penguin Young Readers are leveled by independent reviewers applying the standards developed by Irene Fountas and Gay Su Pinnell in *Matching Books to Readers: Using Leveled Books in Guided Reading*, Heinemann, 1999.

For my son, Taylor—AG

PENGUIN YOUNG READERS
An Imprint of Penguin Random House LLC

Cover art by Rosemary Wells

Copyright © 2017 by Rosemary Wells. All rights reserved. Published by Penguin Young Readers,
an imprint of Penguin Random House LLC, 345 Hudson Street, New York, New York 10014.
Manufactured in China.

Library of Congress Cataloging-in-Publication Data is available.

ISBN 9780515157406 (pbk)   10 9 8 7 6 5 4 3 2 1
ISBN 9780515157413 (hc)   10 9 8 7 6 5 4 3 2

Max & Ruby!
Max's Bug

WITHDRAWN

by Rosemary Wells
illustrated by Andrew Grey

Penguin Young Readers
An Imprint of Penguin Random House

On a morning-glory vine,

Max finds a bug.

He says, "Be mine!"

Its wings are yellow.

Its spots are green.

Max names his bug

Amanda Jean.

Ruby looks over and sees the bug.

"Swat it, Max!" says Ruby. "Ugh!"

Ruby doesn't like the bug.

Max doesn't care.

He gives a shrug.

"He'll bite your feet,

he'll bite your nose!

Get rid of him!

Away he goes!

That bug will sting you

on your ear!"

"No," says Max.

"The bug stays here."

Ruby says, "That bug is such

a silly size.

You cannot even see its eyes.

Bugs make bug juice.

Bug juice stinks!"

But Max doesn't care

what Ruby thinks.

Max says, "My bug's a girl,

like you!

Her name is Amanda Jean.

It's true!

To me, her wings and eyes

look fine.

This bug is happy.

This bug is mine!"

"Well, let's see if she's any fun.

Let's put her on a leaf in the sun."

Amanda Jean begins to fly.

Away she goes! Into the sky!

But she doesn't fly too far.

She flies back into Max's jar.

Max feeds his bug

a worm on a string.

But Amanda Jean won't eat
a thing.

Max wants to teach his bug

a trick.

But Amanda Jean is looking sick.

Max says, "My bug won't hop.

Her spots are red.

I have to put my bug to bed."

"Max," says Ruby, "like any pet, Amanda Jean should go to the vet."

Max puts Amanda in her jar.

They go to the vet.

It's not too far.

The vet squirts bug drops

in a spoon.

She says, "Your bug will be better soon."

"Put Amanda Jean

back on a tree.

Let her fly and let her be free."

Amanda Jean begins to buzz.

She is better than she ever was.

Her six feet tap.

Her spots turn green.

She's the happiest bug

you have ever seen!